名流詩叢
38

在薄層光下

Under the Thin Layers of Light

漢英雙語詩集

於此，細柔草地上
灑佈金黃色晨露觸覺
隨著你的腳印朝向
地平線伸展。諦聽風
以村童的名義在游泳—
鳥群鳴唱，菠蘿蜜枝葉晃蕩；
彷彿愛情，春之笑容—在兩顆心
中間徘徊—正在描繪幸福曙光。

〔孟加拉〕哈珊納·阿布度拉 (Hassanal Abdullah) ◎著

李魁賢 (Lee Kuei-shien) ◎譯

前言

　　哈珊納‧阿布度拉是一種現象。在跨越地理、語言和文學界域方面的能力，於今日孟加拉作家當中，可算是獨一無二。他如此作為，有如海燕飛過風雨飄搖的海洋。他擅長文類，憑超快速度，遠涉十四行詩和史詩；僅僅2014年一年當中，他就出版了四本書，其中有兩本還再版，連書名都令人敬畏。早期詩集展現風格，〈禿鷹很棒〉。另一作品題目暗示詩人年齡與「黑暗」或「以前種種都是創作」。他寫玄想詩，寫歌詞譜樂搶奪得分（雙關語），寫散文押韻，重新配置佩脫拉克十四行詩韻律，創作數百首詩，按照自創的abcdabc efgdefg型式，還有令人震驚的是204頁的宇宙學史詩，他不僅在詩裡信奉新詩學，還有物理學。

他的個人形象和詩作同樣令人印象深刻，腦袋四周披著捲髮，眼睛亮如強力汽車的前燈。我第一次見到他，是在紐約念詩場合，他有摔角選手的胸膛，肌肉明顯在襯衫下方收放。那是二十年前往事。在此期間，我在許多情況下見到他，不僅帶著詩人，還帶來他的鬥士。他是孟加拉詩人胡馬雲‧阿扎德（Humayun Azad）勇敢堅定的後衛。2002年在位於皇后區的寒舍進行孟加拉詩韻問答時，他挑戰另一位孟加拉詩人蘇尼‧岡果普德雅儀（Sunil Gangopdhyay），有更大膽表現！

我很欽佩哈珊納‧阿布度拉，甚至不僅如此，亦未可知。他數學高竿，我卻零分。要談論哈珊納玄學詩，情況同樣；簡直超出我的能力。但我欣賞並

愛讀他的抒情作品，一如他的十四行詩、評論和翻譯。他還編輯一份以孟加拉文為主的詩刊《片語》（*Shabdaguchha*），已歷16年，也許是孟加拉國外唯一此類雜誌。他不屈不撓追求出人頭地，不止是詩，還有身為詩人，就像孟加拉詩人商卜·拉克希特（Sambhu Rakshit）一樣，一年前從文壇神祕失蹤。他把孟加拉和印度西孟加拉邦的詩人聚集在他的雜誌上。如今，隨著本書《在薄層光下》的出版，英文和孟加拉文的讀者都可在不太薄的光層中，探究這位異常優秀的博多河和哈德森河孕育出來的詩人作品。

Jyotirmoy Datta
2015年1月1日

目次

渡輪

此刻我們正在海灣中間

我們解纜時，海濱陰陰暗暗的倉庫
很可能就是製造核彈的祕密設施
整排起重機像金屬長喙兀鷲向前傾斜
拍打渡船船身的海浪是從藍色水域
發來邀請電碼讓我們愉快破譯判讀

在港口，我們忽視在困難蠕動的小艇
右舷有一艘輪船航行太靠近我們時
卻讓一些人驚嚇，但大都是有經驗的渡輪客
很高興向倚靠甲板欄杆的人揮舞手帕

如今燈塔已在地平線消失蹤影
我們在船尾彩繪浮標留下標誌歷史殘骸
我偷瞥天頂，但是海灣上空的蔚藍
不負責任何殺手無人機，渡輪劃開冒泡壕溝
容納三百輛左右汽車和三倍渡輪客

微風用力撥弄我們頭髮，以不清楚的聲音
談論，大海可能只有今天與我們分享

晚間紀事

1

安排好的晚間對手是神

用微笑頷首費力鋪設

        你的花床

真心的情人呀，在事事計畫中

是什麼負擔要誓言或嘆息？

絲毫沒有權利，甚至沒有死亡消息

絲毫無用的是情人的辛勞和計策

我們在下午七八點時要證明什是快樂

如果絕對違背事情的設定

組合崩盤

               百萬強悍聚眾從城市廣場四散

固定農場，滿是奶牛，在氾濫河流中淹沒

一個晚上全毀，驚慌騷動也沒用

確實，到隔天夜裡，你的木屋流失不見

　　　　　　　支柱都被洶湧洪水沖走

晚間，我設計奉獻心力

耗費多年安排的時刻

眼見受到成千腳趾踐踏

我珍貴文辭和韻律的配置

被無心群眾的腳重踩

白天正在樹立一向必然事務

夜裡中斷卻沒有晚間休息

我紅眼面對且硬生生

破成碎片

　　　　我珍惜的晚間

也，破碎啦

　　　　我的心

　　　　　　如此孤單

2

我辛苦操勞18個小時

在夢上加夢

布局晚間

生命卻被突然疾風

吹到無影無蹤

在我懷抱裡

留下冷屍

即刻就會被世界

遺忘

時間搶手

時間搶手。

戰爭、飢餓、永久的公眾恐怖，
懷疑、粗魯爭吵的住所，
疲勞、大量肆虐生命，包含衰頹，
仍然不謬…
時間搶手。

定期解開聲音枷鎖
像瘋子到處瘋狂尋找勝利旗幟，
像狂人把一撮風吹向天空
像傻瓜在失眠黑暗中搞難懂的統計，

因為那麼，也是⋯
時間搶手。

莎士比亞在肥沃土地旁邊跑步
奔向永遠舞文弄字。
要編輯數字的重要性，
費馬從審判庭走到自家住所。
甚至在此之前，伽利略，這為伽利萊的偉大兒子，
透過望遠鏡擴大無可挑剔的思想
把光遍布到全地球，
但盲人還是要走過黑暗監獄。

邊界對面，

住著毗濕奴派詩人——

默圖蘇丹・達達、泰戈爾，

和恢復吹長笛的卡齊・納茲魯・伊斯拉姆

描繪自治，夢想主權土地，

可能的文明，

急急邁向勇敢的追求——

因為那裡，也是⋯

時間搶手。

對異域文化的記憶，

不列顛自滿的不斷折磨，

在分而治之的喜悅中

挖掘，粗糙不衰的墳墓，

度過有秩序的生活──

在血淋淋的非洲和亞洲屋內，

馬蹄達達聲

帶有受辱的自覺…

時間搶手。

從寒冷過去到無言未來，

從帶狀的恐怖叫喊，

冒出人類另一個生命──

頭、肩、心，內外，

逐漸得到強化膽量釋出

禿鷹和公豬的侵略──

朝向明亮的綠地，

整體真相

上路，不倦地走，

因為，迄今為止⋯

時間搶手。

關於手或愈加黑暗

我倏然立起，開始
雙手撕破黑暗
在成功的趨勢中
火炬之光從未瞄準過。

當夜深深降落到我們身上，
當人民持續不斷讚揚——
音樂、舞蹈和高音喇叭
逐漸霸占周圍環境
街頭叫囂充斥我們在途中的
窄門和轉折，時間
在此呻吟，

黑暗被激怒

變得緊密、恐怖和野蠻。

我知道那些殘酷的手

終於會在暗中活躍。

隨著原子彈咳嗽聲成長的手指，

會把生出的細嫩樹枝分散。

性侵案，一個接一個，

加上謀殺和死亡的新聞，

報紙可能也在呻吟中，

但對人民運動沒發生作用，

他們忙著日常生活。

我，也會站起來

會跌倒

失敗、失敗，又失敗

像無益的火炬光；

耐心等待太陽。

我的墓中經驗

去年，我在暑假期間，
為自己挖墳墓。
我想總會有時候
可以好好利用。

讓我告訴你多一些這個故事⋯
我實際上不必要挖新墳，
只要去占用一個舊墓
稍微修繕一番。
坦白說，我是向別人學來的。
占用房屋、土地、語言、國家，
甚至政治，都是偉大的人類實務。

我也在墳墓安裝木門。

除了我，還有誰會安裝這種門！

破土後幾個月內，

我接到電話說可以用啦。

貴在及時…正如他們所說！

所以我搬進去，開鑰，正當黑暗

在牆上到處搖晃實形舌頭時，

孤單已經把我擊潰。

第一個夜晚很難忍受。

身體下方捲起一陣冰冷。

我脫下衣服，塞在下面。

夜長漫漫、恐懼、瘋狂、無情。

黎明時

我出去應自然呼喚——

誰會在墳墓裡設廁所！

悄悄快速完事，

轉回去。

蟑螂、蠕蟲、水蛭

還有更多蠕動爬蟲讓我嚇死啦。

想到蛇，我的血都涼啦。

但是我在墳墓內的恐怖日子

漸漸爬進受折磨的動亂中。

槍擊的雜音

突然，他跳進河裡

突然，他刻意跳進河裡

突然，在那難堪時刻，

　　　他跳進河裡

突然，在那可怕的難堪時刻，

　　　他跳進河裡

突然，帶著討厭的傷口，在可怕血腥的，

　　　難堪時刻，

　　　　　他跳進河裡

洶湧海浪被他的血液染成紅色

霹靂啪啦的槍擊雜音

　　　還在空中震盪—

傷亡的哭聲不斷。

干預叫喊

尖叫聲在我右手掌中迴盪
好像子彈擊中牆上石膏——

那時，是在深夜
高速公路上，離我家門口
幾步之遙，車輛快速彈過⋯
後來，這種折磨已經可以容忍、接受；
與我生活息息相關，如白天和黑夜。
所以干預叫喊，有時，沸沸揚揚
像千年寶貝載翻跟斗⋯
我容易發燒的中毒身體更加惡化了。

還有誰會盡力照顧我的現況？

誰是上等詩人或矮幾公尺

像是目前低能的詩人？

誰寫詩會考慮此事？

如果灰塵、食物、鏟或犁的性質

簡單易行

則全國起義在村莊爆發。

進行如此細微末節的辯論，

筆停止自動書寫。

干預叫喊轉向一邊，

則絲毫無法判斷

愛爾蘭對泰戈爾詩歌的影響

或是印度神話在《荒原》裡的轉換。

這隻手

這隻手

是後現代詩的先決條件。

匆忙拭除現代主義的嚴重塵埃,

對人類遺產的熱心

帶來心思和時刻。

酷、堅固、狡猾──

溫柔和寧靜,

經藝術創作和相互支持。

這隻手

是屬於非洲,

在亞洲朦朧眼界,

強力處理世俗時間。

接受被扭曲世人的護身符
和他們在紐約市搖搖擺擺苟活，
這隻手瞬間轉動
更加快速。

參訪科索沃難民營，
提供瓶裝牛奶
給光身的
又飢餓
又受傷的伊拉克兒童，
坐在孟加拉較不幸
被砷燙傷的家庭主婦旁邊
用淚水洗刷心痛。

這隻手

舉起來對抗核子恐怖

一年52週不停。

星星突然打呵欠

1

我們透過窗戶觀看明亮的世界,感受到光線好像被吸入黑暗中同化。誠然,我們無法發現白天與黑夜—光與暗之間有任何差異。雖然我們對此點沒有費太多思考,但是我們一天兩餐,午夜有性趣,就大喊高興啦,但時間沙沙響編織黑網包圍我們。如果稍有機會回首,什麼都看不到。我們試圖踏步前進,最終,沒有實現,卻陷入腐蝕時代的墳墓裡。

2

我們潛入波動的夜晚。我們潛入快樂的人生競
賽，把自己交給曾經向我們保證過幸福的人。這
些人成為我們的拯救者，像神一樣，儘管他們的
品格不過是一群狗，坐在我們大腦的臥室裡，丟
到他們自己的如意船上。

在銀河焦慮

這是那首詩令人不知所措的本體

那情緒濕潤的眼睛，昨晚

引起我的激情。

坐在駭人房子的

幻夢離合器屋子裡

周圍有高大樹木

陷在蟋蟀唧唧聲中，

我喜愛那光澤四肢的

每次扭曲和轉折

整夜完全失眠。

從趾甲開始，向上滑過

光滑的窈窕身體

到揮舞的噴香水秀髮，

昨夜，

她皮膚的每個細胞都在

我的總體控制下，

好像我是22歲厚顏的野牛

渾身是勁蠻勇

她是18初綻花開。

我全然消失

　　　於她的

　　　　光芒迷宮中。

不，不是夢。

相信我，我通宵忙著

寫新詩作——

深深陷入於

逐步成就

滿懷風的主題，

我遍歷地球上的綠地。

而，今天，邁出去

手攜手，得勝啦。

知否，畢竟，她自己是後現代主義者。

禿鷹好棒

少年時，我看過一些禿鷹。

常棲在聳入高空的巨木樹枝上。

我們往往不加以注意。

他們可能自以為是

上流階級。

所以，我經常看不到牠們過勞的翅膀

和無毛的長脖子。

然而，常常，看到牠們

在高速公路的對面

啄吃公牛屍肉。

我看過一群吵鬧的烏鴉、狐狼，

和溫馴的食肉村狗

在撕吃死母牛的美味乳房。

聽長輩說：「禿鷹不常到本地來，

牠們住在山裡頭。」

偶爾還是下來到我們村莊，在開闊田地，

或在巨大棕櫚樹上。我們年輕人，

遠遠觀看牠們

又懼怕又好奇。

如今，看到禿鷹—很多住在我們周圍。

度著美好生活，享受昂貴食物。

我看到上千、數百萬。

健康，亮麗色彩—

黃、藍、黑和深紅——

正等待機會要用尖嘴撕裂文明。

如今，我看到禿鷹在我們周圍。

鼓舞平靜身體

再寫一首詩，結實且新穎，鼓舞平靜身體。

米爾頓拿起筆，揮動天才雪萊金髮；

而茉莉花甜美的香味

在寧靜空氣中迴蕩

呈現著名光澤——於此，在襯衫上

繡花邊框的褶痕，好像換成

有嚮往海洋的美人魚——永遠快樂的

時候已到。就像哈雷彗星

70年來重新造訪地球——突然

狂喜於逐漸暗澹的夜色。

重組中，文辭急忙並坐在一起，
皮膚拼入皮膚關節─手牽手，
眼對眼，脣在脣上展布愛。
節奏具體表現波動韻律，衝擊
直喻的深刻感性。頭韻微笑
滿足於滿口溫柔果汁，
正如預期天堂之門在東方裂開。

崇拜

詩素動人的手觸及山峰，
印象主義者用舌頭梳理雲的柔髮——
在和風中，世界闔閉老舊、優雅而過敏的
腐蝕性景色，逐漸安於本份。

為達到頂峰，我穿緊鞋攀登更快速，
衝過快樂的本質——我的眼睛上下
閃動——手上的書故意警告吸舔
汗臭味。腳可能會累，但我不會停止。

午夜月落，手牽手與詩素

情話綿綿交心。老太陽

白天坐在那裡，聽鳥鳴聲合唱。

數千年來，沒有什麼隱瞞。

詩鏗鏘的鐲環，在山頂上舞蹈，

擁抱閃爍火光，慢慢沸騰以至狂奔。

降落黑暗

成長中的黑暗牧者四周圍是恐怖的現實⋯

我的活動尚未結束⋯，毒蠍世界正在揚名，將毒牙穿插入血管和骨髓不對等的瘋狂舞蹈裡。

另方面，人民在排隊，有傳染性意識，聲音低低，淹沒在黑暗中，註定要上吊⋯。

被這些想法迷惑之前，我習慣在地板上到處爬行。在這個黑暗已經變成牆壁的密室裡，什麼事都無法理解。我仍然像斷椎的蛇定期在摸索，像討厭的狗不幸斷頸斷腿在狂吠…。

沒入黑暗中…，恐怖至極的時間呀。

罕見的散文書

打開罕見的散文書，

我立刻聽到門口叮噹聲—

果然是你在轉動鑰匙，進來啦。

在極冷的捷牌車[*1]工作環境，

電熱器，急需的朋友—

融入我們肉桂色存在中心。

脫掉冬季外套，

你慢慢變成沒有掩飾如詩。

忘記對空白加以評論，

我盯視你像太陽。

在散文領域，熱帶作物成長—

但冷風開始賦予舒適

正如在本土，可以不管原子彈需要。

如果有人無辜像戈斯瓦米*2

站在人群當中，

有些人可能會急忙嘲笑，

拔他的頭髮，拉他的耳朵。

我們大家，都會有同樣遭遇

在自由地和傳奇性風中。

我們有點孤單和愚蠢

雖然享受到倖存的興奮。

知道天空在

晝夜之間的差異，

你來時，我醒啦

帶著愛上席塔昆度山^{*3}的狂喜。

^{*1}捷牌車（Jalpai），巴基斯坦軍用吉普車，橄欖色，
是1971年孟加拉人最害怕的標誌。
^{*2}喬伊・戈斯瓦米（Joy Goswami），印度西孟加拉
邦著名詩人。
^{*3}席塔昆度山（Shitakundu），位於孟加拉國南方。

西村

也許，是在西村的

老鴇或著名酒鬼；貝多芬式紅眼，

捲髮和百年舊味道的服裝；

然而，刺耳的聲音意味著原子爆炸，

彷彿唯一的超級大國——

披頭族和街上遛狗般的女同性戀運動。

也許，掌握最近的文明標誌

纏在遊蕩客人身上，

在四月下午

出現另一同性戀世代

吸吮時間的汗水。

然後，觀察我們逃跑

到俾路支餐廳[*]
傍徨於檸檬冰黃昏。

莎士比亞的醉酒親戚，
臉曾經像雪萊的白鴿一樣
累積切‧格瓦拉的難民時期。
也許，骨頭，
隨著城市的霓虹燈出現，
測量詩歌迷宮，變得純潔。

在人類及成長文明之間
一打葡萄酒瓶令人目眩。

[*]俾路支（Baluchi）餐廳，在西村。

移民故事

一群移民前進步伐

跟著特赦組織和互聯網。

有些人很聰明,

其他則顯得極為愚蠢。

孟加拉語言

交纏在亞士都、傑克遜高地

和艾倫街的人群閒談中。

在安南雅書店*清爽談話後,

我們兩人急奔地下鐵。

我們的歲月超越夢想的暗室,

高高在上,超越現實最嚴規則

像「棕櫚樹單足獨立…」

讓我單獨離開國家

是我們能容忍的極限。

帶著異鄉的新鮮苦心回家

甚至在夢中，一群不明人士

衝進來，舉起惡毒利爪。

一幫不寬容的人吐得像掛掉。

然後，即使是我們自己的語言也不能好好掌握。

*安南雅（Annanya），孟加拉書店名。

終於令人畏懼的月亮呀

終於，令人畏懼的月亮呀，

你，從淡雲中，來到開闊街道。

正如你所見，現代的綠色轉化，

站在附近歡迎你。夜間玫瑰

快樂爆開。本身充滿愛

輕鬆賦予異國馥郁。

而盲目、不全、無品味的生命

在世紀乾燥的窗口中化身。

從你身上閃現的柔光

令我瘋狂。我明顯領悟到生活意味

月亮和綠色的統合故事──

到今天為止，這些都已經不得見

被塗漆的雲遮蔽。你快樂的日子開啟

我的眼睛。我看到，另外反映雙眼。

無可救藥的夜晚

乳牛在此田園胡亂踐踏，
在其間的女人躺在田壘上，
自稱希妲用尖筆悠然
傳播黑暗。乳牛大膽在她身邊
跳舞，從她裸體上掉下毛髮。
我聽到「可恥！可恥！」
聲音來自人群的各個角落；
怨恨滲透過空氣的疲憊胸懷。

起重機，置放在田園另一邊，
在水平線上輕輕移動白色機翼。
妓女快樂無可救藥的本質
緊貼在稱為白晝的夜晚覆蓋。

夜晚長大，白天長大，二者皆夜晚，
好像白天的花束已經被剪掉。

種族主義暗室

你自從初露創作曙光開始
就留宿在隱藏洞內，你的身體
變胖。有時候，你甚至稍微
有機會，尋找方位從藏身處出現
像蛇。在暴力和殺戮結束時
扭轉脖子，搖晃尾巴，
再度滑回寒冷、安靜、濃厚
暗室。你的眼睛依然邪惡不倦。

我知道，你身處恐怖中心。數世紀來，
你習於浪費爭取機會，保持
面容如此平靜安詳，彷彿是聖人
或是先知。我們感到疲倦、血腥、燥熱
然後就撤退，但還沒打斷你的頭骨。

在薄層光下

在薄層光下聚會，

我們的言辭淹沒在生動祈禱中。

在花園裡，玫瑰和茉莉答應

接受風懷抱的愛，

同時慷慨傳播異國芬芳。

為探索生命，突然長草

在大樹幹下持久——

死者會體認到這種愛嗎？

大黃蜂和蜜蜂成群狂歡——

連池塘、運河和沼澤也笑啦。

鴿子、知更鳥、布穀鳥和鶴更加

靠近彼此樂聲振翅翩翩起舞。

翠綠森林抬眼觀看——

年輕有勁的身心突然閃現光彩。

綠地上房屋第2首

他們知道不知道無關重要。

讓他們知道發生什麼——

讓他們知道是男孩把噴撒

在夢邊緣的愛情花粉變得銳利。

彩色木筏在雲層上舞動。

垂絲柳葉搖動歡迎。

保持看法一致，度過我們時代，

有如在我們心中揮舞愛旗。

握緊我的手，這樣我們可以

踐踏到處累積的懼怕——

我們必須擊潰這路徑的恐怖

走路堅定且強而有力。

看呀，大自然仍然滿眼喜悅，
鳥群仍然在空中展現美麗翅膀。

綠地上房屋第3首

於此，細柔草地上

灑佈金黃色晨露觸覺

隨著你的腳印朝向

地平線伸展。諦聽風

以村童的名義在游泳——

鳥群鳴唱，菠蘿蜜枝葉晃蕩；

彷彿愛情，春之笑容——在兩顆心

中間徘徊——正在描繪幸福曙光。

莫圖莫迪河*，流過村莊，

整天呢喃低語。我仔細

聽均衡動人的祈禱；

開始歡呼和編織希望

用竹子乾草來砌造小屋

讓我們在此耗數小時加數天。

*莫圖莫迪河（Modhumoti），孟加拉國
最長河流之一，也是恆河的分流。詩人
出生於此河岸地方。

綠地上房屋第5首

如果妳絕望地把臉轉過去，

我怎能繪出蒙娜麗莎的形象！

看呀，正當太陽滑入午後

鴿子在電線上鳴唱旋律。

這幅畫可能閃亮如像黎明，

利用畫筆在畫布上添加顏色，

要是還有一兩絡髮黏在妳臉頰。

如果留置空氣中，愛會保持呼吸！

當下午燈光變得安靜時，

一些雲伸展彩色翅膀，

而煮飯花噴出甜味—

滲透白色甜根子草＊田野，

將彩霞被覆全身，

我們會更走近諦聽莫圖莫迪河。

　　　　*甜根子草，草長，開白花。

綠地上房屋第7首

藤花像文辭回到藤莖上；

金色藤蔓荊棘親吻樹葉。

虛張花冠在空中提升魅力——

不，不是熬夜的錯誤。

從月亮身上裝載的神祕

像幸福落到綠地上；

杜鵑繞樹枝跳躍，如同

地球上另一個神奇的早晨笑容。

霧牽著霧的手溜走；

看呀，恢復反射時顏面多麼開朗——

那是糾結在心靈窗框的希望。

把手伸向跨越的時間，

將妳的心靈火炬壓入文辭的核心，

讓荊棘燃燒、燃燒，燒不停。

綠地上房屋第*11*首

青蛙在三月雨中處處合唱，
在泥水中奔跑玩耍。
地面水波沿途沖湧
在風的柔軟邊緣保留痕跡。
循樹幹下來的驚險刺激
在結晶綠地上編織溫馨的下午；
把妳置放在我視線的近距離，
我的心已在最高階段備妥。

把露聚集在一大堆的愛，
閃閃發光，雨流下到指尖
找到想像世界的另一個版圖。
黑暗止步在為光明祈禱，

森林則在漫長狂喜中搖擺——

愛蜿蜒穿過慾望的重要藤蔓。

綠地上房屋第13首

春天的鹿在雲層漫遊，

乳房漲奶，驚訝中眨眼——

精明的頭腦到處跳舞

玫瑰甜香落在團花和無憂樹上。

純粹數學刷新大師心肺，

房屋門口鈴聲閃爍。

想知道破曉時露水多麼濕，

詩立刻在我胸前口袋裡振動。

你跟我走，就近聽我說，就像

綠地穀倉在我臉頰上親吻。

尤加利樹旁的榕樹多麼矮呀？

我心中的甜蜜拱頂多麼高呀？

感情在香蕉枝上揮動面紗，

當妳視線落在我沖浪高潮的眼上。

綠地上房屋第17首

妳拉我的指尖打開妳的胸釦；

秋風吹過狹窄小巷，

培植草加入自然過程—

用藍墨水寫的兩個名字，並列，

十指在搜尋另外十指，

世俗工作室內瀰漫狂熱音樂。

愛的激烈加速扭腰轉動

像船在怒海中顫抖。

月光偷偷潛過窗戶溝縫，

見證實況，好像是昆蟲的

柱頭慢慢伸進來—愛情

向來不平凡—顯露出檸檬葉

香氣。村莊以歌曲和形像，
增加縮影的焦躁算計。

綠地上房屋第19首

走吧，繼續提供金色觸覺。

愛情靜靜坐在生命的倉庫裡。

樹葉和草有愧於泥土，

河流開始在星光反射中竊笑。

稻米、海芋、茉莉和池塘水

在早上和晚上伸展雙臂

呼喚。我也張開紗麗末端

歡迎滿足我心靈空虛的事物。

文辭泅泳跨越過陸地。

蚱蜢在黃昏時斂翅，

鴿群和冬季鳥類

把深愛推入天空口袋。

排排白雲─歡欣又大膽─

輕鬆泅泳，提供冷空氣當禮物。

綠地上房屋第*23*首

終於，我開始走向地獄。

世紀暗礁逐一被擊破。

在孟加拉曆最熱一月天，難忍焦渴

饑饉讓我聽到麻煩的聲音。

全身埋沒在扭扭曲曲的手稿中，

我看到海裡揮舞的污穢潮汐。

雖然海鷗擦掉眼淚，我們時代的

惡棍與深紅殘酷行為，串連在一起。

懷疑扣緊猶豫不決的強大空洞。

剝掉皮膚，磨利可怕的貪婪刀

把文明憤怒踩毀在腳底下。

聲望名牌掛在嫉妒脖子上晃蕩。

在獵豹、蛇和狐狸周遭，

我會因為怕熾熱地獄而畏怯嗎？

綠地上房屋第29首

請把水桶裝滿水，
妳到處灑遍——
災情來時請敲鈴。
破舊房子，妳認不出來，
周圍是芒果和香蕉林
我和情人住過的地方，
玫瑰花盛開的地方
在新太陽召喚下伸枝，

凌亂語辭帶來永恆
疾病——愛情——在風的表皮——
請傾注妳心中的魅力
在地面留下姿影。
可怕的植物，從地面深處
可能再度，揚升永恆的力量。

綠地上房屋第31首

在池塘的透明水中，
吳郭魚仰臉看妳。
周圍大大小小樹木，
熱切期待，片刻閒不住
輕輕瞥一眼妳的臉，
看妳一下─蔚藍天空
悄悄滑到水底下，而風
懶洋洋伸腿坐在草地上。

我怎能說，妳，我命中的愛，
來此房屋只有和我同住？
這片綠林，每一角落都充滿快樂，
親愛的，種類繁多的植物和樹木，

池塘的吳郭魚和最蔚藍的天空——
不都是我的競爭對手嗎?

綠地上房屋第37首

女孩又踏越雪地下來。

我幫她提包包,說「請坐。」

她拂掉手腳沾滿的雪,

望著我說,「親愛的,你好嗎?」

我報以爽快笑容,在她的茶中加糖。

站在我身邊,她把外套掛在衣櫃裡。

我在她眼上輕柔植吻,無聲但情深—

她伸出雙手緊緊抱住我。

離家數千哩,在此城市雪堆內,

我們找到另一種生活。

有時,給我們樂趣;有時,粗魯。

有時,我們心思為家庭而悲傷滾滾。

在這一切當中，愛情向我們伸手，
而群眾卻大爆笑我們無聊。

綠地上房屋第41首

女孩脫掉全身衣服，問道
「愛人呀，告訴我，好看嗎？」
我把她抱緊在胸前，說道
「兩人時世界燦亮；單獨時幽暗。」
這時女孩爆聲大笑起來，
這時小鳥以甜美唧唧聲飛舞，
這時河水以可愛喃喃低語暢流
幸福的天堂湧向我們。

輕柔微風吹著口哨，衝向
牆壁各個角落。草飛，
鴿舞，成對棲止屋頂上；
花卉、水果、樹葉舞蹈，

日光和月輝舞躍

愛情纏綿，永遠糾纏在一起。

綠地上房屋第*43*首

當我們走在街上時，冰
在鹽分地面無聲無息融化──
結晶水毫不猶豫親吻
我們走下斜坡的腳。
我們手牽手離家；
潔白的雲牢牢罩住天空，
冷風像鋸齒在木材上肆虐。
我侵入妳的版圖潛進妳內心。

我們走路時，雲似乎釋出天空，
逐漸減弱冬季的酷寒──
我們雙腳充滿力量，走得更快。
溫柔的愛情藤蔓纏繞我們內心

從我們的關懷和例行激起新春感——
妳的笑容界定我最高潮時刻。

我要吃

我要吃

正在吃，要吃更多

無論得到什麼

　　我確定要吃。

我要吃黎明

　　黃昏

　　　　和黑夜

上班下班回家路上

　　我要在火車和公車上吃

　　我要吃

　　　　無論我經過什麼。

我要吃天堂

　　還有地獄

聰明的傢伙和懶人——

我要吃太陽

　　還有月亮。

我要來來去去

　　隨我願意

輕鬆吃

　　一千場戰爭的軍用喇叭

還有，醜聞，隨時

　　　只要我高興。

我要吃金，吃銀，
眼睛、耳朵和臉
我要吃每一場比賽，
　　　　　　我要。

我要吃宮殿、車輛、
全部豬腸和蟑螂
我要吃偽君子的面具
對，我要吃。

我要吃粗魯的傢伙
　　君王的腦袋

活生生，不是死體，

暴君的命運連腳

　　　　我要吃，

　　　　　　我要。

孤獨星球劇集

我獨處粗略大約46億年。直徑等同仙女座安全距離最近的星系軌道。

我經常進入巨大真空中…。事實上，無言的真空是終極真實，其他一切都是人為的、杜撰的。在浩瀚無際的太空星座──行星、彗星和無數流星的存在範圍內──我小到100兆顆塵粒之一，轉動不停，在我自己軌道內呈23.5度傾斜。

我比孤獨的人更孤獨。

當上帝死啦

當上帝死啦
我會在河裡游泳。
我會踢足球
獲得很多粉絲
為我歡呼。

當上帝死啦
我會在家附近
那森林公園
爬上大樹
殺死所有松鼠
保全我種滿蔬菜的花園。

當上帝死啦

我要吃鮪魚三明治

和五隻油炸蟑螂

作為副食菜單

並請你們傢伙重新思考

關於摩西、耶穌

穆罕默德和克里希納

幾世紀以來

被你們彼此殺掉的人。

當上帝死啦

我要停止寫詩

淑女呀，相信我，

我會和妳上床

連續三天三夜

永不分離。

關於詩人

　　哈珊納・阿布度拉（Hassanal Abdullah），孟加拉裔美國詩人、翻譯家和評論家。首創獨立十四行詩（Swatantra Sonnet），採七七詩行型式和abcdabc efgdefg韻律，用孟加拉語寫200多首。出版42本書，包括 304頁的史詩《*Nakhatra O Manusar Prochhad*》（Ananya出版社，2007年初版，2017年再版），根據幾種科學理論，闡述人類與宇宙間的關係。《詩選》第二版於2014年出版。編過《20世紀孟加拉詩選》（孟加拉文，Mowla

出版社，2015年）。三本雙語詩集《孟加拉氣息》（*Breath of Bengal*, CCC出版社，2000年）、《在薄層光下》（*Under the Thin Layers of Light*, CCC出版社，2015年）和《獨立14行詩》（*Swatantra Sonnets*, 孟加拉文與英譯，Feral Press＆CCC出版社，2017年），由亞馬遜網路經銷。著作《詩韻》（*Kobiter Chhanda*, 孟加拉學術院出版，1997年，第2版Mowla出版社，2011年），自1997年起一直是孟加拉大學參考文獻。2016年應邀參加中國四川國際絲路詩歌節，獲荷馬歐洲詩藝術獎章。2013年以新創十四行詩型獲拉布亥（Labubhai）基金會獎，於2007年獲皇后區桂冠詩人獎。

2000年以來，一直是三州地區眾多場地的矚目詩人。翻譯過波特萊爾、阿赫瑪托娃、史丹利·庫尼茨、希克默德、特朗斯特羅默、尼卡諾爾・帕拉、辛波絲卡、傑拉德・斯特恩，和更多詩人作品為孟加拉文，以及超過35位孟加拉詩人作品為英文。其本身詩作被譯成九種不同語文，並選入數部世界詩選集。現任紐約市立高中數學教師，1998年起擔任國際雙語詩刊《片語》（*Shabdaguchha*）編輯。2017年4月達卡Puthiniloy出版社刊印《哈珊納・阿布度拉：詩人航海家》（*Hassanal Abdullah: Poet Voyager*）雙語（孟加拉語和英語）作品選集，包括評論、訪談和信件，慶祝他50歲生日。

　　2019年獲皇后區藝術委員會翻譯補助，並應邀參加希臘哈爾基斯（Chalkida）詩歌節，於此結識漢譯者李魁賢。《詩集成》（孟加拉文）第一卷最近在達卡出版。

關於譯者

　　李魁賢，1937年生，1953 年開始發表詩作，曾任台灣筆會會長，國家文化藝術基金會董事長。現任國際作家藝術家協會理事、世界詩人運動組織副會長、福爾摩莎國際詩歌節策劃。詩被譯成各種語文在日本、韓國、加拿大、紐西蘭、荷蘭、南斯拉夫、羅馬尼亞、印度、希臘、美國、西班牙、巴西、蒙古、俄羅斯、立陶宛、古巴、智利、尼加拉瓜、孟加拉、馬其頓、土耳其、波蘭、塞爾維亞、葡萄牙、馬來西

亞、義大利、墨西哥、摩洛哥等國發表。

出版著作包括《李魁賢詩集》全6冊、《李魁賢文集》全10冊、《李魁賢譯詩集》全8冊、翻譯《歐洲經典詩選》全25冊、《名流詩叢》38冊、李魁賢回憶錄《人生拼圖》和《我的新世紀詩路》，及其他共二百餘本。英譯詩集有《愛是我的信仰》、《溫柔的美感》、《島與島之間》、《黃昏時刻》、《存在或不存在》和《感應》。詩集《黃昏時刻》被譯成英文、蒙古文、俄羅斯文、羅馬尼亞文、西班牙文、法文、韓文、孟加拉文、塞爾維亞文、阿爾巴尼亞文、土耳其文，以及有待出版的馬其頓文、德文、阿拉伯文等。

曾獲韓國亞洲詩人貢獻獎、榮後台灣詩獎、賴和文學獎、行政院文化獎、印度麥氏學會詩人獎、吳三連獎新詩獎、台灣新文學貢獻獎、蒙古文化基金會文化名人獎牌和詩人獎章、蒙古建國八百週年成吉思汗金牌、成吉思汗大學金質獎章和蒙古作家聯盟推廣蒙古文學貢獻獎、真理大學台灣文學家牛津獎、韓國高麗文學獎、孟加拉卡塔克文學獎、馬其頓奈姆・弗拉謝里文學獎、祕魯特里爾塞金獎和金幟獎、台灣國家文藝獎、印度普立哲書商首席傑出詩獎、蒙特內哥羅（黑山）共和國文學翻譯協會文學翻譯獎、塞爾維亞國際卓越詩藝一級騎士獎。

Foreword

Hassanal Abdullah is a phenomenon. Among today's writers from Bengal, he is perhaps unique in his ability to cross geographical, linguistic and literary borders. He does so with the ease of a petrel crossing storm-tossed seas. With awesome speed, he masters literary genres as far apart as the sonnet and the epic; in the space of 2014 alone, he published four books, including two second editions. Even the titles of his books inspire awe. An early collection was styled, *Vultures Are Doing Well*. The title of another work implies that the poet is of the same age as of Darkness or What Was Before There Was Creation. He writes metaphysical poems, tosses out by the score (pun intended) lyrics to be set to music, essays on meter,

rearranges the Petrarchan rhyme scheme for the sonnet, instead producing hundreds of them conforming to an abcdabc efgdefg pattern of his own, astounds us with a 204-page epic on cosmology, in which he not only espouses a new poetics but also physics.

His personal appearance is as impressive as his poetry. His head is surrounded by a halo of curly hair. His eyes are as bright as the headlamps of a powerful automobile. When I first encountered him at a poetry reading in New York, he had the chest of a wrestler, with muscles visibly coiling and uncoiling under his shirt. That was twenty years ago. In the intervening period, I have seen him in many situations that brought out not just the poet but also the fighter in him. He has been a brave and steadfast defender of Humayun Azad. Even more daring perhaps was his challenging Sunil Gangopdhyay to a Q&A on Bengali prosody at my home in Queens in 2002!

There is much about Hassanal Abdullah that I admire, even more that I do not understand. He is good at mathematics—in which I score a zero. Perhaps the same thing happens when I come to Hassanal's metaphysical poetry; I might just be out of my depth. But I appreciate and enjoy his lyric work, as also his sonnets, and his critical essays, and his translations. He has also edited a chiefly-Bangla poetry magazine for 16 years, *Shabdaguchha*, perhaps the only such magazine outside

Bengal. He has been indefatigable in his championship of not just poetry, but poets, as in the case of Sambhu Rakshit, who disappeared mysteriously from the literary scene a year ago. He has brought Bangladesh and West Bengal poets together on the pages of his magazine. Now, with the publication of this book, *Under the Thin Layers of Light*, both English and Bangla readers will be able to examine in not-so-thin layers of light the works of this phenomenal Padma-Hudson poet.

Jyotirmoy Datta
1 January 2015

Ferry Ride

Now we are right in the middle of the bay

When we cast off, the somber warehouses on the waterfront

could well have been secret facilities for the making

    of nuclear bombs

and the row of cranes leaned forward like metal Gyps

    indicus

The waves tapped on the hull of the ferry an invitation

from the blue waters in a code we joyously deciphered

On our port we overtook a boat wriggling between

    hills on the run

On the starboard a ship cruised past us close enough

to give a few of us a fright, but most being experienced
    ferry riders
happily waved kerchiefs at the people leaning on the
    rails of its deck

Now the lighthouse disappears beneath the horizon
We leave in the stern painted buoys marking historic
    wrecks
I steal a glance at the sky overhead but that blue over
    the bay
is innocent of any killer drones, and the ferry cuts a
    bubbly furrow
with three hundred or so autos and thrice as many riders

The breeze runs an eloquent finger through our hair,
speaking in
an unknown tongue the sea might have shared with us
just for today

Translation from the Bengali by Jyotirmoy Datta

Evening Chronicle

1

Enemy of arranged evenings is the Lord

laying waste your bed of flowers

with a smile and a nod

What weight has a vow or sigh

earnest lover, in the scheme of things?

With no rights at all, not even to news of the dying

of no use at all is a lover's toil and planning

of what we will PROVE for delight at eight, or seven

If that's absolutely against the set of things

corporations crumble

million-strong rallies disperse from city squares,

solid farms, complete with cows, vanish in the ravenous

    river

No use kicking up a fuss over a ruined evening

For sure, as night follows day, your hut disappears

    when the posts are washed away in a raging flood

The evening I designed with such devotion

the years I spent arranging moments

I see a thousand toenails trampling them to dust

My precious arrangements of words and rhymes

pounded by the feet of thoughtless multitudes

The day is setting as it always must

The night breaks with no pause for evening

I meet it with eyes red and raw

Broken to pieces

      my precious evening

Broken, too,

     my heart

         so lonesome

2

Eighteen hours I toiled

piling dream on dream

Arranging the evening

its life blown away

by a sudden gust

leaving in my arms

its cold corpse

soon to be forgotten

by the world

Time Seizes the Hands

Time seizes the hands.

War, hunger, perpetual public terror,

suspicion, careless conflicting habitation,

fatigue, enormous sweep of life, including decay,

still infallibly ...

Time seizes the hands.

Regularly unfastening the chain of sounds like a lunatic

madly searching flags of victory everywhere,

throwing away handfuls of wind to the sky like a maniac,

unfathomable statistics of sleepless darkness like a fool,

because then, too ...

Time seizes the hands.

Beside the fertile land, Shakespeare runs

towards eternity taking up the alphabets.

The importance of numbers be edited,

Fermat goes to his own abode from the assizes.

Even before that, Galileo, the great son of Galilei,

enlarged his impeccable thoughts through the telescope

spreading light all over the earth,

but the blind man still walks through the prison of darkness.

On the other side of the boundary,

dwell the Vaishnava Poets—

Madhusudan Dutt, Rabindranath Tagore,

and, retuning on his own flute, Kazi Nazrul Islam

draws Swaraj, dreams of a sovereign land,

possible civilization,

and hurries toward courageous pursuit—

because there, too ...

Time seizes the hands.

The memory of alien culture,

unremitting torment of the British conceit,

digging, the crude ageless grave

in the joy of divide and conquer,

lives an ordered life—

in the houses of blood-bathed Africa and Asia,

the clip-clopping of horses' hooves

with assaulted conscience ...

Time seizes the hands.

From the chilling past to the unspoken future,

from the banded ghastly shout,

emerges another life for human beings—

head, shoulder and heart, inside and out,

gradually getting the strengthened guts to unleash

the invasion of vultures and boars—

and toward the illuminated greenery,

Total Truth

walks on, untiringly walks,

because, until now ...

Time seizes the hands.

Translated from the Bengali by Siddique M. Rahman

About the Hands
or the Growing Darkness

I suddenly stood and started to tear

the darkness with both hands

that the torchlight never targeted

in a successful trend.

When the night was deeply descending on us,

when people burst into bigoted exaltation—

music, dance, and high-pitched horn

were increasingly occupying the surroundings,

and the street howling suffused our tips and turns

on the way, as time moaned,

right there,

the darkness infuriated,

became dense and dire and wild.

And I knew those cruel hands would

eventually be active in the dark.

Those nails, grown with the atomic gurgle,

would scatter the tender branches of birth.

Rapes, one after the other,

and with the news of murder and death,

newspapers might also be moaning,

but nothing would happen to people's movement,

and their busy day-to-day life.

And I, too, would stand up

and would fall

and fail and fail and fail

like the futile torchlight;

and would patiently await the sun.

Translated from the Bengali by the poet

My Experience in a Grave

Last year, during the summer vacation,

I dug a grave for myself.

I thought I would have good use of it

some time.

Let me tell you more about the story ...

I actually didn't have to dig a new grave,

I just had to occupy an old one

and then fixed it up a little.

To be frank, I learned it from other people.

Occupying homes, land, language,

states, and even politics is a great human practice.

I also installed a wooden door to the grave.

Who else would install such a door but me!

Within a couple of months after the break,

I got a call for using it.

A stitch in time ... as they say!

So I entered, turning the key, as the darkness

wove its tangible tongue all over the wall,

aloneness crumbled me.

The very first night was unbearable.

There was a freezing cold furling beneath my body.

I took off my clothes and squeezed them under me.

The night was long, fearful, frantic, and merciless.

At daybreak,

I went out responding to my natural call—

who would ever make a loo in a grave!

Silently finishing it fast,

I went back in.

Roaches, worms, leeches

and many more creepy-crawlies scared me to death.

Thinking of snakes, my blood grew cold.

But my gruesome days in the grave

gradually crawled into crucified convulsions.

Translated from the Bengali by the poet

The Cacophony of the Gunfire

Suddenly, he jumped into the river

Suddenly, he managed to jump into the river

Suddenly, at that devastating moment,

       he jumped into the river

Suddenly, at that fearsome, devastating moment,

       he jumped into the river

Suddenly, with a horrible wound, at that fearsome, bloody,

       devastating moment,

          he jumped into the river

The surging waves turned red with his blood

The cacophony of the clattering gunfire

        was still vibrating in the air—

and the constant cry of the wounded and dying.

Translated from the Bengali by the poet

Intervening Outcry

Screams echoed in the palm of my right hand

as if a bullet hit the plaster on a wall—

Then, it was deep at night

on the highway, a few steps away

from my door, the vehicles shooting quickly by ...

Lately, this torture has become tolerable, acceptable;

it has clung to my life, like day and dark.

So the intervening outcry, sometimes, drifts beyond

like a millennium baby somersaulting ...

my fever-prone poisoned body aggravates.

Who else takes great care of my condition?

Who is senior or measured a few meters short

like a poet of lower caliber for the time being?

Who writes poetry taking this into account?

If the nature of dust, food, spade or plough

is simple and easy,

then national uplifting breaks out in the village.

Taking up such a trivial debate,

the pen stops scribbling of its own accord.

The intervening outcry turns aside,

then it's at all useless to judge

the Irish influence on Tagore's songs

or the conversion of Indian myth in "The Waste Land."

Translated from the Bengali by Siddique M. Rahman

This Hand

This hand

is a postulate of a postmodern poem.

Removing the drastic dust of modernism hastily,

it brings minds and moments

to the heart of human heritage.

Cool, robust, crafty—

gentle and tranquil,

artistically composed and mutually supportive.

This hand

is of Africa,

at the hazy sights of Asia,

a vigorous treatment of temporal time.

Accepting amulets of the wrenched human beings

and their staggering survival in New York City,

this hand turns momentarily

further apace.

Visiting the refugee camps of Kosovo,

supplying bottles of milk

to the naked

hungry

lacerated children of Iraq,

sitting beside the arsenic-scalded

less-fortunate housewives of Bangladesh

and washing out the heartache with tears,

this hand

rises up against the nuclear terror

fifty-two weeks a year.

Translated from the Bengali by Siddique M. Rahman

A Sudden Yawn of a Star

1

Staring at the luminous world through the window, we feel the light as if it were assimilated in the absorbing darkness. Indeed, we cannot find any differences between the day and the night—light and dark. Though we don't think about this a lot, though we shout happiness getting two meals a day and sex at midnight, the raucous time weaves its dark nets around us. If we get a slight chance to look back, we can't see anything. We try to pace forward, but eventually, without realizing it, we fall into a grave of corroding age.

2

We dive into the waving evening. We dive into the cheerful race of life and hand ourselves over to people who once promised us happiness. People—who become our rescuers as if they were the gods, though they had the quality of becoming nothing but a bunch of dogs—sitting in the bedchambers of our brains casting away on their own wishful vessels.

Translated from the Bengali by the poet

Anxiety in the Milky Way

This is the bewildering body of that poem

whose emotion-drenched eyes, last night,

made me passionate.

Sitting in a dream-clutch room

of an astounding house

surrounded with tall trees

and trenched in crickets hum,

I relished each and every twist and turn

of her lustrous limbs

completely sleepless throughout the night.

Starting from the toenail, gliding up

through the smoothness of the slender body

to the sway of her perfumed hair,

last night,

every cell of her skin was

in my total control,

as if I were a brazen bison of

twenty-two, a vibrating valiant, and

she was an unveiled virgin of blooming eighteen.

I entirely dissolved

into her

luminous labyrinth.

No, it's not a dream.

Believe me, I was up for the whole night

with my new poem—

plunging deep into

the success in the cascade

filled up with the proposition of the wind,

I permeated through the fortunate greens of the earth.

And, today, walked out

hand-in-hand, victorious.

You know, after all, she herself is a postmodernist.

Translated from the Bengali by Siddique M. Rahman

Vultures are doing well

In my boyhood, I saw a few vultures.

They used to sit on the giant branches of the sky-high trees.

Usually, we did not notice them.

They might have thought of themselves

to be in the upper class.

Therefore, I could not often see their extravagant wings

and long hairless throats.

Once in a while, however, they were seen

on the other side of the highway

eating the flesh of dead bulls.

I saw a group of quarrelsome crows, jackals,

and gentle carnivorous village dogs

eating the delicious breasts of a dead cow.

"Vultures do not come to the locality often,

they live in the mountains," commented our elders.

Still, they occasionally came down to our village, in

    the open field,

or on the big palm trees. We, the teenagers,

watched them from a distance

with a mix of fear and curiosity.

Now, I see vultures—lots of them living around us.

They lead a gorgeous life eating expensive food.

I see thousands, millions of them.

They are healthy, brightly colored—

yellow, blue, black, and crimson—

waiting for a chance to tear at civilization with their

    sharp beaks.

Now, I see vultures all around me.

Translated from the Bengali by the poet

Stirs the Smooth Body

Again a poem, firm and fresh, stirs its smooth body.

Milton picks up his pen, swings the golden hair

of Shelley, the genius; and the sweet scent

of Jasmine roams around in the calm air

in renowned luster—here, in the plaits of

the chemise-embroidered border, as if, trading

a mermaid with oceanic dreams—it is the time

for eternal joy. It's like Haley's comet

revisiting the earth in seventy years—a sudden

rapture of the darkening night.

In a reunion, words rush to sit together side-by-side,

skin merges in the skin joint—hand gets in hand,

eyes in eyes, and lips spread love on lips.

Rhythms embodied in the waving rhymes, jolting

the deep sense of simile. Alliteration smiles in

satisfaction with mouth full of tender juice, as the

expected door of heaven cracks open in the East.

Translated from Bengali by Purnima Ray

Worship

The eloquent hand of poetry touches the mountain peak,

its impressionist tongue soothes the cloud's silky hair—

in the soft wind, the world rests its old, tempered and

    prickly

sight of erosion and gradually gets its own share.

To get to the top, I climb up faster wearing tight shoes,

rushing through the essence of joy—my eyes bob

up-and-down—books in hand willfully warn sucking

the smell of sweat. Feet may be tired but I don't stop.

Descending the moon at midnight, holding hands

engaging in erotic talk with poetry. The age-old

sun, sitting there in the daylight, chorused by bird-songs.

Thousands of years pass by, nothing is untold.

Jingle poetry's bangles, dance at the mountaintop,

to embrace the flickering fire, simmering and racing up.

Translated from the Bengali by the poet

Sinking Darkness

Ghastly reality all around the herd of growing darkness ...

My activities are not completed yet ... but the scorpion-world is exalting by implanting its fangs in a disparate frenzied dance of vein and marrow.

On the other hand, people are queued, in an infectious conscious, limited voice, submerged in the darkness destined to be hanged ...

Before being captivated by such thoughts, I used to crawl on the floor, here and there. Nothing is intelligible in this cell where the darkness has turned

into walls. Still I fumble about in regular intervals like a snake with a broken spine, shouting like an abominable dog ... hapless with broken neck and legs.

Immersing darkness ... ghastly, monstrous exhausted Time.

Translated from the Bengali by Siddique M. Rahman

A Rare Book of Prose

Soon after opening a rare book of prose,

I heard a clinking at the door—

you, indeed, turning your key, came in.

In the *Jalpai* occupation of indefinite cold,

electric heaters, friends in need—

infused in the center of our cinnamon existence.

Taking off your winter coat,

you slowly became naked as poetry.

Forgetting the comment on the margin,

I stared at you like the sun.

In the land of prose, the hot crop grew—

but the cold wind began to give comfort

as it did in the native land, careless of the atomic demand.

If someone innocent as Joy Goswami

would stand in a crowd,

a few might come rushing to ridicule,

by picking at his hair and dragging him by the ear.

We, all of us, at times, were treated the same

in the land of liberty and legendary wind.

We were a bit lonely and foolish,

though we enjoyed the excitement of survival.

Knowing the sky-difference

between day and night,

when you come, I wake up

with ecstasy of *shitakundu*-love.

Jalpai: olive color. Pakistani army jeeps were olive, which
          was the most feared sign for Bengalis in 1971.
Joy Goswami: a poet from West Bengal, India.
Shitakundu: A mountain in the southern wing of Bangladesh.

Translated from the Bengali by the poet

West Village

Maybe, a pimp or a well-known alcoholic

of the West Village; Beethoven-red-eyes,

sticky hair and a century-old smelly dress;

yet the harsh voice signifies the atomic explosion,

as if the only Super Power—

the Beatniks and the street-dog-like Lesbian movement.

Maybe, holding the latest sign of civilization

tangling in the body of floating tourists,

in an April afternoon

emerges another gay generation

sucking the sweat of time.

Thereafter, observing our escape

to the *Baluchi*

crawls the lemon-ice evening.

A drunken relative of Shakespeare,

whose face was once like Shelley's white pigeon,

accumulated with the refugee-time of Che Guevara.

Maybe, the bone,

emerging with the neon light of the city,

measured the maze of poetry, becoming pure.

A dozen wine bottles dazzled between

the human race and its growing civility.

Baluchi: a restaurant in the West Village.

Translated from the Bengali by the poet

A Story of Immigrants

A group of immigrants pace forward

with Amnesty and Internet.

Some are very clever,

while others show their extreme foolishness.

And the Bengali words

reel around the chat of people clusters from Astoria,

Jackson Heights, and Allen Street.

After a fresh talk at *Annanya,*

we two rush to the subway.

Our days are beyond dream's dark doom,

high up, well above reality's roughest rules

like "the palm tree on one foot ... "

Leave me alone to leave my country

is the limit of our tolerance.

Returning home with the fresh pain of the foreign land

even in our dreams, a group of unknown people

rushes in, raising their vicious claws.

A gang of intolerance throws spit like kicks.

Then, we do not grasp well even our own language.

Annanya: Bengali book store

Translated from Bengali by Nazrul Islam Naz

At last the Awesome Moon

Out of the shreds of cloud, at last, you,

the awesome moon, have come onto the open street.

The modern translation of green, as you can see,

stands close to welcome you. The rose of night

bursts out with joy. Its body full of love

bestows at ease an exotic perfume. And

a blind, incomplete, infinite taste of life

incarnates at the century's dry window.

The tender light sparking out of your body

maddens me. Clearly, I realize that living means

a unified story of the moon and the green—

all of which have been out of sight up to this day,

covered by a lacquered cloud. Your joyful days open

my eyes. Two more eyes, I see, reflected in them.

Translated from Bengali by Purnima Ray

Incurable Night

Disorderly graze the cows in this field,

women in between lie down along the ridge,

a self-declared Sita spreads darkness at her

leisure with a pointed pen. The cows dance

boldly by her side dropping their fleece

on her naked body. "Shame, shame," I hear

coming from every corner of the crowd;

hatred oozes down piercing the tired breast of air.

Cranes, seated on the other side of the field,

lightly move their white wings on the horizon.

Incurable essence of prostitute-happiness

clings to the lid of the night named as the day.

The night grows, the day grows, though both are nights,

as if the day's bouquet of light has already been cut.

Translated from the Bengali by Purnima Ray

The Dark Chamber of Racism

You have nested in hidden holes since the beginning

of the very dawn of creation. Your body

grew fat. At times, while you got even a slight

chance, you looked for trends and emerged

like a snake from your hideout. At the end of violence

and killing, twisting your neck and shaking your tail,

you again slid back into the cold, quiet, and copious

dark chamber. Your eyes were still vicious and tireless.

You are in the center of terror, I know. For centuries,

you skillfully spun the wheel of conflict, keeping

your face so calm and quiet, as if it were of a saint

or prophet. We get tired, bloody, and burnt, and then
retreat, but still fail to break your skull.

Translated from Bengali by Purnima Ray

Under the Thin Layers of Light

Assembling under the thin layers of light,

our words drowned in vital prayer.

In the garden, rose and jasmine, engaged

in receiving love from the bosom of the wind,

while unselfishly spreading exotic scent.

In search of life, suddenly arose grass

that was long under the big tree trunk—

would the dead ever realize this love?

Hornets and bees swarmed in ecstasy—

the ponds, canals, and marshes smiled, too.

Pigeons, robins, cuckoos, and cranes came

closer to each other's music fluttering their wings.

The green forest lifted its eyes and looked—

The young exuberant heart suddenly shone in luster.

Translated from Bengali by Purnima Ray

A House on the Green 2

It does not matter if they know it.

Let them know whatever happened—

let them know that the boy sharpened

love's pollen sprinkled on the edge of a dream.

The colorful raft danced over the cloud.

Tamarisk leaves quivered to welcome it.

Keeping eye on eye, we passed our time,

as if we waved the flag of love in our heart.

Hold on to my hand so that we can step

on fears accumulated, here and there—

we have to crush the horror of this path

while walking firm and strong.

Look, nature still blinks with joy,

birds still set their beautiful wings in the sky.

Translated from Bengali by Purnima Ray

A House on the Green 3

Here, on the soft grass, sprinkles

the golden touch of morning dew

as your footprints stretch out

toward the horizon. Listen to the wind

swimming in the name of the village boy—

birds sing, jackfruit branches shiver;

as if love, Spring's smile—lingering between

two hearts—is drawing the dawn of happiness.

Modhumoti, flowing beyond the village,

murmurs all day long. Carefully, I listen

to its well-balanced attractive *arati*;

and begin cheering and weaving hope

to build a hut with bamboo and hay

where we would spend hours and days.

Modhumoti: a river, on the bank of which the poet was born
arati: prayer.

Translated from Bengali by Purnima Ray

A House on the Green 5

If you move your face aside in despair,

how can I draw the Mona Lisa figure!

Look, on the telephone wires, doves singing

melodies as the sun slides into the afternoon.

The drawing might sparkle like the daybreak,

as the brush adding colors onto the canvas,

if a strand or two of hair sticks to your cheeks.

Love keeps breathing if it's bestowed in the air!

When the afternoon light becomes still,

and a few clouds stretch colorful wings,

and *sandhya-malati* sprays sweet scent—

penetrating the white *kash* field,

wrapping dusk's light all over the body,

we will come closer to hear *modhumoti*.

sandhya-malati: a kind of evening flower
kash: long grass with white flowers.
modhumoti: a river.

Translated from Bengali by Purnima Ray

A House on the Green 7

Rattan flowers return on the stem as words;

thorns of the golden vine kiss the leaves.

Garlands of talk raise their charm in the air—

no, not a mistake staying up through the night.

Mount of mystery from the body of the moon

comes down on the green as happiness does;

the cuckoo jumps around the branches, as

another miraculous morning smiles on the earth.

Fog slips away holding the hands of fog;

look, what clears its face in retrieving reflection—

it's hope entangled on the edge of mind's window.

Spread your hands towards the spanning time,

press your heart's torch into the word's heart,

let the thorn burn, burn, and burn forever.

Translated from Bengali by Purnima Ray

A House on the Green 11

Frogs choir all over in the *Asher* rain,

run around the muddy water and play.

The ground water-wave rushes its way

keeping traces at the soft edge of the wind.

Thrills that come down through the tree trunk

weave a gentle afternoon on the crystalline green;

to place you at the close range of my sight,

my heart is ready at the highest stage.

The love that deposited its dew in clusters,

sparkling, rains down on the fingertips

to find another realm of imaginary world.

Darkness stands still in praying for light,

as the forest swings in extended ecstasy—

love winds through the vital vine of desire.

Asher: the 3rd month of the Bengali calendar

Translated from Bengali by Purnima Ray

A House on the Green 13

The spring-deer roams around the clouds,

breasts full of milk, eyes blink in surprise—

the crafted mind dances all around, while

the sweet aroma of roses sits in *kadam, saraca.*

As pure math refreshes the lungs of a master,

the bell twinkles at the entrance of the house.

To know how wet is the dew when the dawn breaks,

poetry instantly vibrates in my chest pocket.

You walk with me to hear me close, as the granary

of the green draws kisses on both my cheeks.

How short is a banyan tree next to a eucalyptus?

How high is the sweet dome of my mind?

Emotion swings its veil on banana branches,

as your eyes fall on my eyes surfing up the tide.

> kadam and saraca: trees native to Bangladesh, the latter also
> called asoka (Sorrowless Tree).

Translated from Bengali by Purnima Ray

A House on the Green 17

You open your breast-button at my fingertips;

the autumn wind rolls through the narrowing lane,

and the cultivated grass joins in its natural course—

two names written in blue ink, lie side by side,

ten fingers search for the other ten in them,

an earthly studio is embedded with wild music.

The rage of love speeds up in twist and turn

as the boat trembles in the middle of a roaring sea.

Moonlight picks through the window gutter,

witnessing the instance as if the stem-head

of a creeper slowly penetrates—love has

never been ordinary—it exposes the aroma

of lime-leaves. The village, its song and images,

increase the nerve-reckoning at the epitome.

Translated from Bengali by Purnima Ray

A House on the Green 19

Go, go on to offer the golden touch.

Love is quietly seated in life's storehouse.

Leaves and grass bestow their debt for soil,

rivers begin to giggle in stars' reflection.

Paddy, arum, jasmine, and pond water call

stretching their arms in the morning and in

the evening. I, too, have spread my sari's end

to welcome whatever sat

isfies my mind's emptiness.

The words swim across the land.

Grasshoppers shrug off their wings at dusk,

flocks of pigeons and winter birds push

their deep love into the pockets of the sky.

White rows of cloud—jubilant and bold—

swimming at ease, offering cold air as a gift.

Translated from Bengali by Purnima Ray

A House on the Green 23

Finally, I've started walking towards Hell.

The shelves of the century are broken one by one.

In the hottest day of *Baishak,* unbearable drought

and famine made me listen to the tiresome voices.

My body is engulfed in the distorted scripts,

as I see the dirty tides waving in the sea.

While seagulls wipe their tears, the villains

of our time chain them with crimson cruelty.

Doubt fastened the mighty hollow of hesitation.

Peeling off the skin, sharp dreadful greedy knives

smashed civilization angrily beneath the feet.

The ornament of fame dangles on jealousy's neck.

In this neighborhood of cheetah, snake, and fox,

will I be shrinking in fear of blazing Hell?

Baishak: the first month of the Bengali calendar, when the monsoon arrives after a long drought.

Translated from Bengali by Purnima Ray

A House on the Green 29

Bring buckets full of water, please,

sprinkle them all over up to your heart's content—

if disasters ever come ringing the bell.

The old tattered house, you wouldn't recognize,

surrounded by mango and banana groves

where my love and I used to reside,

where flowers bloomed on the rose

branches at the beckoning of the new sun,

where disheveled words brought an eternal

sickness—love—on the wind's skin—

please pour the temptation of your heart

and leave scratches of gesture on the ground.

Deep from the ground, the devastating plants

might, once again, rise to everlasting power.

Translated from Bengali by Purnima Ray

A House on the Green 31

In the transparent water of the pond,

a tilapia raises its face to look at you.

Trees, large and small, surrounding it

eagerly await, impatient all the while

to catch a slight glimpse of your face,

to take a glance at you—the blue sky

silently slides down under water, and the wind

sits on the grass lazily stretching its legs.

How can I say, you, love of my life,

have come to this house to live only with me?

This green forest, every corner full of mirth,

this widening variety of plants and trees,

tilapia of the pond, and the bluest sky—

are not all of them my competitors, dear?

Translated from Bengali by Purnima Ray

A House on the Green 37

Treading across the snow, the girl comes down again.

I help her with her bags and say, "Please have a seat."

Shaking the mound of snow off her hands and feet,

she looks at me, and says, "How are you, dear?"

Drawing a quick smile, I add sugar to her tea.

Standing by me, she hangs her coat in the closet.

I plant a soft kiss, soundless but deep, on her eye—

she stretches her hands to hold me tight.

In this city of mounds of snow, thousands of miles

away from the homeland, we find another life.

Sometimes, it offers us fun; sometimes, it's rude.

Sometimes, our minds swell in sorrow for home.

Amidst all this, love stretches out its hands to us,

while crowds burst with laughter at our leisure.

Translated from Bengali by Purnima Ray

A House on the Green 41

Taking all of her dress off, the girl asks,

"Tell me, my love, how do I look?"

Pressing her tight to my chest, I say,

"The world lights up in two; darkens in one."

Then the girl bursts into laughter,

then the bird dances with a sweet chirp,

then the river runs in lovely murmur,

as the heaven of happiness rushes in us.

The soft wind whistles, pushing on

corners of the wall. The grass dances,

the pigeons dance, sitting in pairs on rooftops;

the flowers, fruits, leaves of trees dance,

the daylight and the moon dance

where love tangles and entangles forever.

Translated from Bengali by Purnima Ray

A House on the Green 43

As we walk down the street, the ice

silently melts on the salty ground—

the crystal water does not hesitate

to kiss our feet as it travels down the slope.

We left home holding hands;

The cloud's whiteness firmly covers the sky,

a cold wind rushes like a saw on a log.

I draw into your realm to dive inside you.

As we walk, the cloud seems to unleash the sky,

gradually blunting the sharpness of winter—

our feet stirred with strength to walk even faster.

The tender vine of love entwining our hearts

stirs spring freshness from our cares and chores—

your smile defines my highest moment of joy.

Translated from Bengali by Purnima Ray

I will eat

I will eat

Eating now and will eat more

Whatever I get

    I will eat for sure.

I will eat the dawn

      the dusk

        and the dark

On the way to work back to home

    I will eat on the train and bus

    I will eat

        whatever I pass.

I will eat Heaven

        and Hell

Wise guys and the loon—

I will eat the sun

        and the moon.

I will come and go

        as I wish

Eating the bugle of

        a thousand battles at ease

scandals, too, whenever

        I please.

I will eat silver, gold,

Eyes, ears, and the face

I will eat each and every race,

    I will.

I will eat palaces, coaches,

Guts of all swine and roaches

I will eat the mask of the hypocrite

Yes, I will eat.

I will eat peasants

  the monarch's head

Alive, not the dead,

The tyrant's fate with feet

I will eat,

I will.

Translated from Bengali by Dhananjoy Saha

An Episode of a Lonely Planet

My loneliness is roughly about 4.6 billion years old. Its diameter is as great as the closest galaxy—orbiting at a safe distance from Andromeda.

Often I enter into a huge vacuum... In fact, the unspoken vacuum is the ultimate truth, everything else is artificial, fabricated. Within the vast infinity of the spatial constellation—planets, comets, and within the existence of innumerable meteors—I am as little as one of the 10^{14} of a grain of dust, spinning forever, tilting at twenty-three-and-a half degrees inside my own orbit.

I am lonelier than man alone.

Translated from the Bengali by the poet

When God is Dead

When God is dead
I will swim in the river.
I will play football
and get a lot of fans
to cheer for it.

When God is dead
I will climb the big tree up
in Forest Park
near my house
and kill all the squirrels
to save my garden full of vegetables.

When God is dead

I will eat a tuna fish sandwich

and five fried cockroaches

as a side order

and ask you guys to rethink

about Moses, Jesus,

Muhammad, and Krishna

for whom you have been killing

each other for centuries.

When God is dead

I will stop writing poems

and believe me, my lady,

I will be in a bed with you

for three consecutive days and nights

and will never be separated.

Translated from the Bengali by the poet

About the Poet

Hassanal Abdullah, a Bangladeshi-American poet, translator, and critic. He introduced a new sonnet form, *Swatantra Sonnet*, seven-seven stanza pattern and abcdabc efgdefg rhyming scheme, more than 200 of which he wrote in Bengali. He is the author of 42 books in various genres, has written a 304-page epic, *Nakhatra O Manusar Prochhad* (Ananya, 2007, 2nd edition 2017), where, based on several scientific theories, he illustrates relations between human beings and the universe. The second edition of his *Selected Poems* was published in 2014. He edited the *Twentieth Century Bengali Poetry* (Bangla Text, Mowla, 2015). His three bilingual poetry collections, *Breath of Bengal* (CCC, 2000), *Under the Thin Layers*

of Light (CCC, 2015) and *Swatantra Sonnets: Bengali with English Translation* (Feral Press & CCC, 2017) are available at Amazon.com. His book, *Kobiter Chhanda* (Bangla Academy 1997, 2nd ed. Mowla, 2011) has been a university reference text in Bangladesh since 1997. In 2016, he was invited to attend the *International Silk Road Poetry Festival in Szechuan,* China where he was awarded the Homer European Medal of Poetry & Art. He also received the Labubhai Foundation Award (2013) for his innovative sonnets, and was the honorable mention of Queens Borough Poet Laureate in 2007.

He has been a featured poet in many venues on the tri-state area since 2000. He translated Charles Baudelaire,

Anna Akhamatova, Stanley Kunitz, Nazım Hikmet, Tomas Tranströmer, Nicanor Parra, Wislawa Szymborska and Gerald Stern and many more into Bengali, and more than 35 Bengali poets into English. His own poetry has been translated into nine different languages. He contributed to several world poetry anthologies. Mr. Abdullah is a NYC high school math teacher and the editor of an international bilingual poetry magazine, *Shabdaguchha*, since 1998. *Hassanal Abdullah: Poet Voyager*, a bilingual (Bengali-English) anthology about his work, including critical essays, interviews and letters, was published in April, 2017 from Dhaka by Puthiniloy Publication on his 50th Birthday.

Hassanal received a translation grant from the Queens Council on the Arts and was invited to the 2nd International Poetry Festival, Chalkida, Greece, in 2019. The first volume of his *Collected Poems* (Bengali Text) was recently published in Dhaka.

About the Translator

Lee Kuei-shien (b. 1937) began to write poems in 1953, became a member of the International Academy of Poets in England in 1976, joined to establish the Taiwan P.E.N. in 1987, elected as Vice-President and then President of it, and served as chairman of National Culture and Arts Foundation from 2005 to 2007. Now, he is Vice President for Asia in Movimiento Poetas del Mumdo (PPdM) since 2014, the organizer of Formosa International Poetry Festival. His poems have been translated and published in Japan, Korea, Canada, New Zealand, The Netherlands, Yugoslavia, Romania, India, Greece, USA, Spain, Brazil, Mongolia, Russia, Latvia, Cuba, Chile, Nicaragua, Bangladesh, Macedonia, Turkey Poland, Serbia, Portugal, Malaysia, Italy, Mexico and Morocco.

Published works include *"Collected Poems"* in six volumes, 2001, *"Collected Essays"* in ten volumes, 2002, *"Translated Poems"* in eight volumes, 2003, *"Anthology of European Poetry"* in 25 volumes, 2001~2005, *"Elite Poetry Series"* in 38 volumes, 2010~2017, and others in total more than 200 books. His poems in English translation include *"Love is my Faith"*, 1997, *"Beauty of Tenderness"*, 2001, *"Between Islands"*, 2005, *"The Hour of Twilight"*, 2010, *"20 Love Poems to Chile"*, 2015, *"Existence or Non-existence"*, 2017, and *"Sculpture & Poetry"*, 2018. The book *"The Hour of Twilight"* has been translated into English, Mongol, Russian, Romanian, Spanish, French, Korean, Bengali, Serbian, Albanian and

Turkish, and yet to be published in Macedonian, German, and Arabic languages.

Awarded with Merit of Asian Poet, Korea (1993), Rong-hou Taiwanese Poet Prize, Taiwan (1997), World Poet of the Year 1997, Poets International, India (1998), Poet of the Millennium Award, International poets Academy, India (2000), Lai Ho Literature Prize, Taiwan (2001) and Premier Culture Prize, Taiwan (2002). He also received the Michael Madhusudan Poet Award from the Michael Madhusudan Academy, India (2002), Wu San-lien Prize in Literature, Taiwan (2004), Poet Medal from Mongolian Cultural Foundation, Mongolia (2005), Chinggis Khaan Golden Medal for 800th Anniversary of Mongolian State,

Mongolia (2006), Oxford Award for Taiwan Writers, Taiwan (2011), Award of Corea Literature, Korea (2013), Kathak Literary Award, Bangladesh (2016), Literary Award "Naim Frashëri", Macedonia (2016), "Trilce de Oro", Peru (2017), National Culture and Arts Prize, Taiwan (2018), Bandera Iluminada, Peru (2018)and Prime Poetry Award for Excellence by Pulitzer Books, India (2019), Literary Award for Translation from Association of Literary Translators of Montenegro（Udruzenje knjizevnih prevodilaca Crne Gore）（2020）, International Award "A Knight of the First Order of Noble Skills in Poetry" from "Raskovnik" Literary and Artistic Association, Smederevo, Serbia（2020）.

He was nominated by International Poets Academy and Poets International in India as a candidate for the Nobel Prize in Literature in 2002, 2004 and 2006, respectively.

Contents

語言文學類　PG2406　名流詩叢38

在薄層光下 Under the Thin Layers of Light
——漢英雙語詩集

原　　著／哈珊納‧阿布度拉（Hassanal Abdullah）
譯　　者／李魁賢（Lee Kuei-shien）
責任編輯／林昕平、陳彥儒
圖文排版／楊家齊
封面設計／蔡瑋筠

發 行 人／宋政坤
法律顧問／毛國樑　律師
出版發行／秀威資訊科技股份有限公司
　　　　　114台北市內湖區瑞光路76巷65號1樓
　　　　　電話：+886-2-2796-3638　傳真：+886-2-2796-1377
　　　　　http://www.showwe.com.tw
劃撥帳號／19563868　戶名：秀威資訊科技股份有限公司
　　　　　讀者服務信箱：service@showwe.com.tw
展售門市／國家書店（松江門市）
　　　　　104台北市中山區松江路209號1樓
　　　　　電話：+886-2-2518-0207　傳真：+886-2-2518-0778
網路訂購／秀威網路書店：https://store.showwe.tw
　　　　　國家網路書店：https://www.govbooks.com.tw

2020年9月　BOD一版
定價：270元
版權所有　翻印必究
本書如有缺頁、破損或裝訂錯誤，請寄回更換

國家圖書館出版品預行編目

在薄層光下：漢英雙語詩集 / 哈珊納.阿布度拉(Hassanal
  Abdullah)著；李魁賢譯. -- 一版. -- 臺北市：秀威資訊
科技, 2020.09
    面；　公分. -- (語言文學類；PG2406)(名流詩叢；
38)
  BOD版
  譯自 : Under the thin layers of light
  ISBN 978-986-326-841-3(平裝)

869.3351   109011806

讀者回函卡

感謝您購買本書，為提升服務品質，請填妥以下資料，將讀者回函卡直接寄回或傳真本公司，收到您的寶貴意見後，我們會收藏記錄及檢討，謝謝！
如您需要了解本公司最新出版書目、購書優惠或企劃活動，歡迎您上網查詢或下載相關資料：http:// www.showwe.com.tw

您購買的書名：＿＿＿＿＿＿＿＿＿＿＿＿＿＿＿＿＿＿＿＿＿＿＿

出生日期：＿＿＿＿＿年＿＿＿＿＿月＿＿＿＿＿日

學歷：□高中 (含) 以下　　　□大專　　　□研究所 (含) 以上

職業：□製造業　□金融業　□資訊業　□軍警　□傳播業　□自由業
　　　□服務業　□公務員　□教職　　□學生　□家管　　□其它＿＿＿＿

購書地點：□網路書店　□實體書店　□書展　□郵購　□贈閱　□其他

您從何得知本書的消息？

　□網路書店　□實體書店　□網路搜尋　□電子報　□書訊　□雜誌
　□傳播媒體　□親友推薦　□網站推薦　□部落格　□其他＿＿＿＿＿＿

您對本書的評價：(請填代號　1.非常滿意　2.滿意　3.尚可　4.再改進)

　封面設計＿＿＿　版面編排＿＿＿　內容＿＿＿　文／譯筆＿＿＿　價格＿＿＿

讀完書後您覺得：

　□很有收穫　□有收穫　□收穫不多　□沒收穫

對我們的建議：＿＿＿＿＿＿＿＿＿＿＿＿＿＿＿＿＿＿＿＿＿＿＿

＿＿＿＿＿＿＿＿＿＿＿＿＿＿＿＿＿＿＿＿＿＿＿＿＿＿＿＿＿＿＿

＿＿＿＿＿＿＿＿＿＿＿＿＿＿＿＿＿＿＿＿＿＿＿＿＿＿＿＿＿＿＿

＿＿＿＿＿＿＿＿＿＿＿＿＿＿＿＿＿＿＿＿＿＿＿＿＿＿＿＿＿＿＿

11466
台北市內湖區瑞光路 76 巷 65 號 1 樓

秀威資訊科技股份有限公司　　　收

BOD 數位出版事業部

....

（請沿線對折寄回，謝謝！）

姓　　名：＿＿＿＿＿＿＿＿＿　年齡：＿＿＿＿　性別：□女　□男

郵遞區號：□□□□□

地　　址：＿＿＿＿＿＿＿＿＿＿＿＿＿＿＿＿＿＿＿＿

聯絡電話：(日)＿＿＿＿＿＿＿＿＿＿　(夜)＿＿＿＿＿＿＿＿＿＿

E-mail：＿＿＿＿＿＿＿＿＿＿＿＿＿＿＿＿＿＿＿＿＿＿